Ajia

Reine-Aurore Agbodan

Copyright © 2020 Reine-Aurore Agbodan
ISBN: 9798672297392
Imprint: Independently published
All rights reserved.

DEDICATION

To my true love and best friend my husband Sylvain Agbodan:
Thank you for always listening to my endless stories.
To my family who always inspires me to be creative and brave.
 Family Peyandane, Ello, Ngongang, Ntetmen, Ngoko and Petteng.
And to all my friends for supporting me and giving me the most
precious feedback.

CONTENTS

Ajia

I do not like weddings. I was feeling a pain in my chest, like someone was poking at my heart with needles. I desperately needed some water, two deep breaths from my inhaler and I should be fine. I was still wondering why I was always torturing myself with so many questions. This was not my wedding after all. It sure wouldn't be now, not at twenty-three years old. I was still young. Although I was aware some of my girlfriends have tied the knot already. The truth was, I was not ready! I was still trying to figure out exactly who I would like to be. Pondering to define what precisely I was looking for in my future.

Yes, I really would love to get married one day but I was too scared to take that step. My tastes, feelings and expectations seemed to change every second. Why did I feel this extreme pain during weddings though? I seemed to be OK with the subject of marriage but then witnessing the union always filled me with hurt.

Everyone wants to be loved. I got it…What I didn't understand is why love seemed to come with pain for me. I saw that pain on too many women's face when I was growing up, all for a man! I didn't want to experience a similar situation ever. I needed to learn how to trust. I had to hold tight to the hope that good men do exist. Men who are capable of loving, taking care and protecting their family 'until death do them part.' I strongly needed to believe that.

Feeling much better and relaxed, I stepped out of the restroom.

"Hello, feeling better?" Said a tall guy dressed in a beige suit. He was putting himself together as if he has been waiting for a while.

"Yes, I'm feeling better, thank you."

"Glad to hear. I can't bear to see tears on a pretty face. And when you ran out…"

"Oh, this! It was nothing, I'm always emotional at weddings. These tears… it's just an expression of joy!" I answered feeling a bit embarrassed. I thought I was fine when I last checked in the mirror, wasn't I?

"I understand. It was a wonderful ceremony. Quite emotional. By the way, I'm Anthony," he said stretching his hand towards me.

"I'm Ajia"

"Nice to meet you Ajia. Unfortunately, I can only stay for the ceremony! I hope to see you again Ajia! I am glad you're feeling better now. Take care."

"Thank you, that's really thoughtful." I said before he winked at me and walked out.

Beige suit...not really my thing but I like the feeling this meeting leaves me with. He seems very caring for a stranger which he might always be since I don't know anything more about him; except his first name. I've never met someone like this bef…Actually I did.

This encounter with Anthony brought back memories: someone I walked into in the past, a meeting that led to a very complicated story. Oh well, let the past be past and hopefully the future will be…bright. Look at me trying to make a rhyme or rather failing flatly!!!

Liam

This reception was the best ever! I'm not saying this because Janelle is my girl. The truth is, I haven't had so much fun in a long time. The groom, Andrew, had selected the music. This mix of old school and current jam was just fabulous. As the music slowed down, I proceeded to make my way back to my table. My best friend Allan, the bride's brother had already saved me a dance earlier. It was funny to see old school "uncles" making their move...

They attended weddings to seek young women like me for a tight close-up dance that lasts forever.... It was usually hard to turn them down as the majority saw me 'growing up'! This made the whole situation awkward and repulsive...

"Cranberry juice and a Rose" uttered the voice of a young man. "Red is still your favorite colour, right?"

My heart jumped at the sound of his voice. Could it be? He continued:

"I saw you at the ceremony earlier, but I didn't want to interrupt your conversation. I would have gotten a bird of paradise, but they only had roses in the back garden."

"Liam" I shouted. Happy, though surprised, to see him again. "Nice to hear you still you remember my favorite flowers, but this rose is beautiful too. Too bad you had to steal it! Thanks for the drink."

"You are welcome, Ajia. How are you doing?"

His words hold so much meaning behind them. We stared at each other for a while before I responded.

"I'm doing well. Not exactly where you left me but not too far either. And you?"

"I know…I wanted to call you, Ajia. When you moved to Europe I didn't know if you would still read my emails..."
This man never really took the time to know me at all .Or he might have a short memory.
"Anyway, so much time had gone by… You know I really would love to see you again, to chat. We could go to Malibu; I remember how you loved that place hmm... can't remember the name but I can take you there with my eyes closed. Anyway, let me know, I have the same number. Actually, I'll call you. Enjoy your evening, Ajia!"
"Thanks, Liam. Goodbye!"

As Liam was leaving, I noticed that my best friend Allan was furious. His eyes were screaming 'baby girl, not again please'. I went to sit at the table, and just stayed quiet holding Allan's hands. I was too shaken to say a word. Allan was also silent, staring at the beautiful bride, processing with sadness the fact that his only sister was starting a new life away from him.

Rooftop

"So, when are you guys meeting?" Allan asked. I was sitting with my best friend Allan on the rooftop of a downtown building in Los Angeles, where this California heatwave was a little bit more bearable. We spent hours at the fashion district trying to find the best outfits for an upcoming photo-shoot. It was a well-earned time to chill in one of our favorite spots in the city. This bar gave a magnificent view of the Downtown skyline. I loved sitting on their plush sofa by the fireplace on the outdoor patio. I had a swim once in their crystal-clear swimming pool during a Spring break party Allan's father threw for us in our first year of college. I still remember it: Allan and I were expecting a return ticket to Cancun, but his father and my uncle wouldn't have it. The party was our gift that's it. Little did they know, we had our back up plan and when Allan's grandmother handed us those flight tickets they were red! When Allan and I set our mind on something, it was always bound to happen.

The photo shoot was scheduled to take place in two days. Allan and I had planned everything. From finding models to the venue and filling out the required paperwork. Allan wasn't happy about the outfits, especially the accessories we received. Fashion was a world we shared together from a young age. Allan was skilled in the designing aspect, and me the photography. We spent most of our time last year gathering ideas and taking pictures of Europeans' unique fashion style. Allan was blessed with a tremendous opportunity: an internship in a prominent designer house. I followed him with my camera. I remembered that I had to promise my uncle I would enroll in Law school for me to have that sabbatical year for myself. It was an amazing year and we both got to travel and experience work in the fashion industry. At first, I was just doing some modelling to make money, so I wouldn't depend on my uncle too much. Then, after a photo shoot in Germany with the photographer being sick on the second day, I got my first shot at photography. The house, Devante, was so impressed with my work that they hired me as the assistant photographer. I learned so much since. Today I was back in LA, living my first year at UCLA Law school. I have to admit I was loving it! But while Law had my brain, Fashion held my heart. Moreover, like Allan always says, we will need some legal expertise when we'll launch our own design company. Allan was pursuing fashion design at the University of California in LA. This photoshoot was our personal project. It was a chance to feature our work in an online fashion magazine. Since we already have our brand, this would be a great opportunity to promote it and get some feedback from high fashion critics and professionals. Our brand was a combination of inspiration we got from our European experience and Allan's unique fashion vision. I had come up with a variety of scenes indoors and outdoors and I was quite proud of the venues I was able to book for us. Allan and I had spent our time talking business. We also talked about my upcoming exam at the law school. Now that we could finally relax around some cocktails and snacks, Allan was eager to cut through the chase.

"So when are you guys meeting?"

"I don't know! Liam said he would call me. You know what that means."

"Uncertainty! And?"

"I don't expect anything from him anymore. I won't deny still having feelings for him, but I can certainly live without him."

"Amen to that, Ajia! You already know my opinion about the whole situation with you and Liam. However, I trust you know what you doing and I will support you."

"Thank You bestie!"

"It's alright, I just want you to know I'm here for you if you need me. Do you think you and Liam will get back together?"

"I don't know. I don't want to think about it because getting back with him would be like cheating on myself. All the hurt and lies, I can't just forget it and jump back into it."

"I have a strong feeling you will get back with him."

"I'm afraid I might. You know how much the flesh is weak... Honestly, bestie, I loved that man! Do you understand?"

"I do! That's why I'm so upset about the idea of you and him getting back together. Mostly him playing touch and go again! But if he hurts you again, he's a dead man..."

"Allan! Come on!"

"I'm just saying."

"Alright! Let's talk about you now. How is it going with Miss Nigeria?"

"Quite well. I'm taking it easy you know. We are talking, a lot. I invited her to your uncle's barbecue. Please don't scare her away."

"I won't. However, I would love to ask her a few questions... just to check the sister out, you know. See if she's good for my brother."

"Here you go! I know you Ajia. Please don't even try and scare her!"

We both laughed.

Anthony

It would not be a proper summer season without my uncle's barbecue party. It's a family reunion where my family and our close friends would catch up on what was happening in each other's life! Sometimes, for the nosy ones, in other people's life. Uncle Eddie had also invited the Acton and the Johnson families. Both couples were retired and had entered our social circle not too long ago. My family was still getting to know them. They had grown-up children, some of them were married, and a few were still enrolled in college. I only met three of them so far. I met Kay and Amber at a bridal shower three months ago. We started getting to know each other better when we went horseback riding with some mutual friends two weeks ago and since then we were texting, checking on each other regularly. I also met their cousin Ross at a basketball court on Huntington Beach where I play from time to time. Yes, both families were related. I noticed that the girls did not join in today. I went to say hello to Ross who was chatting with my cousin Carlton and a couple of other people. One of them looked just like him but shorter.

"So you know Ross and Antwine?" Anthony asked.

What a nice surprise, I didn't know Uncle Eddie had invited Anthony, the guy I met at the wedding recently. I didn't even know he knew him. Anthony was about my size, well with my heels on. He had this charismatic smile. I was fascinated by his attractive laugh. Anthony was quite buff with his broad shoulder and muscular arms. His soft eyes made me think he was a sensitive guy. I could tell he was quite charming, and I wondered why I had not noticed him before!

"Hello Anthony, quite a surprise to see you here! Yes, I met Ross a while ago. We play basketball from time to time.

However, I don't think I know Antwine!"

"It's nice to see you Ajia! I knew we would meet again. Ross and Antwine Johnson are my cousins!"

"Ah! I see! Wow I have to ask aunty and uncle exactly how many children they have, I keep meeting up a new sibling, cousin!"

"You are so funny! Yes we are quite a big family!" Anthony added with a laugh. He continued:"I'm being extremely rude: How are you? Can I offer you a drink?"

"I am well thanks. No thank you for the drink, Anthony. I'm covered." I said pointing to my glass sitting on the shelf.

"So Ajia, you play basketball?"

"Yes, I do. Just for fun though! I played for the team when I was in high school. Then other hobbies plus studies took over. Now I join the guys on the court from time to time when I'm not too busy. What about you? Do you play?"

"No, not really. But I like sport. I regularly go to the gym, the usual."

"Sounds cool! I love the gym, I couldn't give that up!"

"Really? We should go to the gym sometimes, where do you go?"

"For the gym? Home. My uncle has a nice set up in the garage."

"That's handy. Well, I like to go to a friendly gym in Downtown Long Beach. You should come sometimes."

"Sounds good."

Anthony went on to introduce me to the rest of his family, the ones present at the party. It was a very nice gathering with some Afrobeat and Caribbean Music. Many rushed to the dance floor. As the midnight hour was getting near, I noticed some people had gone home. Few grown folks had set in the living room with my uncle's selection of whiskey, talking about basketball. My cousin Carlton, some of his friends as well as Allan and his girlfriend were sitting in the backyard. There, Uncle Eddie had created over the years a proper backyard oasis with flagstones, stone pillars and a redwood hot tub, with overflowing water, set in a deck. My uncle would proudly highlight that the tub was a 'Western Red Cedar tub.' A more recent highlight was the stone fine pit surrounded by built-in seating. Aunty Elaine had also added her touch with a set of Teak Adirondack loveseat, a rocking sun lounger made with Acacia wood and her amazing gardening work. Uncle Eddie was working so hard designing living spaces for his clients it was only fair his own house would be the most beautiful example of his work. I joined the group of youngsters, listening to their conversation. Allan's girlfriend was quite animated in the discussion; I didn't pay much attention though. At some point, my thoughts drifted like the bubbly water from infinity tub and I replayed my earlier encounter with Anthony over and over in my head. I was still in the clouds when Anthony showed up again for a chat. He asked me to join him to a party the next day. Allan was quick to remind me we already had plans. I was quite impressed when Anthony then asked for my number, I mean I know men do it all the time, but there and then in front of my family and friends most of whom he barely knew. It was brave.I have to say bold men don't come by so often. Or maybe I've only met the sneaky ones... That night, I was pondering about the events of the day, like I always do while trying to sleep. Then, I noticed I had received a text from

Anthony. I was quite surprised given the time. He was 'making' sure he had the right number and wanted to confirm our plan to work out.   I was looking forward to work out with Anthony. To be honest I wanted to get back to the gym for a while! When Anthony asked me about working out together, I pretended to be working out regularly. The truth was I used to but lately I barely had time. I didn't know what to make of Anthony. He was being nice, sweet… And chatting with him was quite refreshing. I replied and turned my phone off after reading his last words: 'Sweet dream beautiful.'

Move your body

"Ji! You changed your outfit so much this morning! I wonder if you really going to work out or do something else!"

"Darling leave her alone!" said Aunty Elaine.

"Thank you, aunty. Anthony should be here any minute now" Uncle Eddie was right. I changed about 4 times already. I don't know why I was feeling overly self-conscious instead of just being my usual self. Anthony was a nice guy beside, it's not like this was a date. Far from it, we were going to sweat! As I reached out to grab my gym bag, the doorbell rang.

"Hello Anthony!"

"Morning Ajia! You look nice, are you going somewhere fancy?"

Now, I was embarrassed.

"Sorry! It this too much? I have a pair of shorts in my gym bag if needed..."

"I'm joking! You look nice Ajia! Your outfit is perfect for our work out. You might want to leave the gym bag. Just take your water. We are going to run from here to the dojo."

"You serious? Didn't you say the gym was by the marina?"

"Yes indeed. Why? Are you afraid of a challenge?"

"No, not at all. Let me put my sneakers on then." I said leaving him in the living room where Uncle Eddie and Aunty Elaine were finishing their coffee.

"Hello young man!" My uncle said in a nice and loud voice.

"Hello uncle. How are you this morning? And you, aunty?"

"I'm very well. Would you like some coffee? I made some scones to go with it. A family recipe. Please have some!"

"Thank you, aunty, I'm fine. I only drink my shake before a work out. Maybe I will get some when we get back.

"Ok, I'm ready." I said fixing my iPod on my left arm.
"What's that drink?"
"Oh, it's my strawberry protein juice. It's delicious, want to try?"
"Err...nope! I love strawberries, but I can't stand it as a flavor."
"I have chocolate as well, in the car."
"I thought we were running to the dojo."
"Yes, we are. The car is parked over there."
"Oh good, at least we won't have to run back!" I whispered.
"What did you sayy?"
"Nothing. Alright let's go. Bye guys!"
"You sure you don't want your cousin to go with you Ajia?"
"No uncle. Carlton is still sleeping anyway. Next time!"
I understood my uncle's concerns; he was always looking out for me. Running down the beach was exhilarating. We passed all sorts of people, from the soccer mom hurrying to get her kids to school to the businessman blurting stock market numbers into his phone. My favorites were the tourists with their backpack and digital camera wowing at the Californian scenery. Focusing on these people helped me endure the pain. My body was clearly telling me I was not in good shape. I had not been running lately and I just realized that I had not stretched before engaging in this race. I was praying Anthony wouldn't notice that I was struggling to keep up. I was so fortunate he was listening to music through his headphones. I turned the music up! Glad that I selected a powerful and rhythmic playlist. Each beat was pushing my legs forward and soon the marina was appearing before us. Anthony tapped me on my arm and pointed at a small building a block away from the wa-

ter. We changed direction and slowed down to enter the parking lot.

"Here, take this" Anthony said, grabbing a bottle of water from his car. He must have put it in the freezer last night because a block of ice was floating inside the bottle.

"Thank you. This is so refreshing!"

"You impress me Ajia, You are quite a runner. It was hard keeping up with you."

"You are being either extremely nice or just naive, I am out of breath! But thank you for the compliment!   Is that the dojo you told me about?"

"Yes, let's check it out. We can do some stretching exercises and maybe follow up with some weight if you up to it." he said as we proceeded to the door.

Crepes, Monsieur?

"I'll meet you later this afternoon for the French Connection meeting… You don't need to go over your French lesson, Allan! They all speak English… You are joking, right? French connection is just their brand name! If we can bag a photoshoot deal with them, it would be awesome! Great income potential and wonderful credentials for our business…I still can't believe they want you, my best friend, to design some of the clothes for them. 'The Allan collection by French Connection'! I can already picture it…I know that's not actually your brand's name, excuse you, 'our' brands name! Alright, let me calm down…I can't stay on the phone too long but let's meet up at 1pm to go over our proposal. Ok, bye babe!"

"You just met the guy last week and you are already booed up on the phone. Man, Ajia you are moving fast!" said my cousin Carlton as he emerged from I don't even know where, and was now looking for something in the fridge.

"Who do you think I was talking to? For your information, I was talking to Allan. And get your head out of the fridge. We are having breakfast in the front room, here take this. Now don't spoil my mood because I'm having a great morning so far, and I sure want to keep it that way!"

"I see. Dang! You even made crêpes (French pancakes), and the whole European breakfast deal! That is indeed a good start of the day!" added Carlton.

"Yes but don't touch anything yet, I invited Anthony for breakfast. He should be here soon."

"See, I knew things were progressing with the dude. So tell me Ji, could he be 'the' one?"

"I don't know." I answered, feeling confused for a while plus I wasn't sure if Carlton was being serious or still joking. "Anthony is just a friend! And would you please go put some proper clothes on!"

"Come on now, Ajia. You know I'm on my school break. I was waiting for this moment all term so I could walk around in my pyjamas all day!"

"Come on Carlton, go get dressed before our guest arrives", said Aunty Elaine.

"OK, I gotta be ready anyway, in case the dude wants to take you somewhere, Jia. I got to keep an eye on him!"

"This dude has a name and you know it". I shouted as Carlton ran up the stairs to his bedroom.

My younger cousin Carlton could be so annoying sometimes. Even though I found it very touching the way, he remembers little things about me. I told him about finding the 'right guy' some years ago when we foolishly used to play truth and dare. He could be so overprotective sometimes. Between Carlton, Allan, and Uncle Eddie, I was bound to remain single for the rest of my life if I didn't get things under control. Anyway, that would do for now. After all, I was not in anything serious with the 'dude'. Not yet.

  "Ajia, the crêpes are fabulous! I have always thought it was a larger version of pancake, but it does have a different taste".

"Thank you, Anthony."

"So, do you have plans for today?"

"Yes. My business partner and I have an important meeting this afternoon. Then I'm going to go on campus to work on a case with some classmates."

"A case? Already?"

"Not like that. We have this class where we go over past cases and recreate them in groups. We need to do a lot of research on past and current laws and policies. The goal is to see how the outcome of these cases would be different in the light of modern law."

"That's very interesting. You seem really passionate about it too."

I could see my uncle smiling with pride.

"I enjoy it so far." I answered, with a smile.

"She's got another passion though" added Carlton, mouth full of pancakes.

"Oh yeah? May I please know what her passion is? Or is it a family secret? asked Anthony.

"I don't know if I can say," replied Carlton, "ask Ajia."

"No, it's not a secret. I'll show you." I said taking out my laptop.

Thinking about Anthony's charm and kindness, I wondered how many hearts he had broken. I had learned my lesson in the past and was determined not to rush into anything but safeguard my heart. Later in the day as I was on my way to meet Allan, I got a notice from my phone. Looking at the screen, I could see that it was a text message from Liam. I ignored it for now as I wasn't ready to deal with it yet.

Down Memory Lane

The rest of the day went very well. I would have said smooth, but Allan and I were so anxious before the meeting with French Connection. We met at an English pub an hour before to go over everything again! We also had the chance to grab something to eat. The waiter suggested a 'pint of beer' which was very enticing in this hot weather. Maybe it could have helped drown our stress. But, I opted for an elderflower mocktail. As my drink arrived I remembered Liam's text. What's the link between an alcoholic beverage and my ex-boyfriend? You may ask. I wish I could speak about it freely, but it is way too embarrassing. It was one of those moments in your life that you desperately try to forget. Oh yes, did I mention Liam used to be my boyfriend? You may have guessed it I'm sure. So yes, I did try to forget some things about my ex-boyfriend, things I don't like to revisit but just to give you the full picture of our history I will: I honestly forgot many details of that evening. However, I do remember how awful I felt. That night, I had consumed alcohol with some kind of pain killers. Don't get me wrong now, I don't take drugs nor binge drink. Actually, I rarely drink; drinking just a glass of wine puts me to sleep so It's not something I would usually order if I want to enjoy my evening out! But on that morning, I remembered waking up with horrible period cramps, so I spent the rest of the day taking pain killers, with an empty stomach, I know that's the worst thing to do but I couldn't hold any food down. I had a date planned with Liam in the evening and I really didn't want to cancel so I just took my pills, slept and prayed I would feel better by 6pm. The painkiller eventually worked. I was up and ready for my date. We went to a Mexican Restaurant. The Restaurant had a special offer on their margaritas. Liam loved the margarita and suggested I should try it…just to loosen up a bit. I remember not feeling too comfortable. Liam was already taking shouts and was more animated with people in the restaurant than with me. Was I boring? Is it why I agreed to have another drink even though I didn't really want to? What followed is a bit blurry for me… I just remember the room going upside down, we had gone somewhere else but I could only hear people shouting. I didn't want to be there any more but even that decision wasn't in my control. I felt wet all of a sudden, this big shower, was I in a shower? It couldn't be…yes that's it, I was running in the street and it had started to rain… Anyway, at the beginning of that night, I felt safe being with Liam and now I was alone in these streets. I don't remember many details about what took place, but I know Liam let me down big time. With time, I realized I also let myself down! What happened that night had negatively impacted our relationship. Not to mention I almost got into big trouble with my family who still adores him. I had to cover for him; I made the awful decision to lie for someone who had let me down just because I loved him. I still have that vivid memory of my best friend, Allan, picking me up in the rain. I've always had him on speed dial somehow. He took me home that night .We had to stay in the car for a while just so I could get myself together before facing my uncle and aunt. They had no idea where I was and I had never stayed out so late without calling

or texting. Allan didn't ask any question, although I could feel he wanted to. Especially where was Liam, why did he let me get to that state and how come he wasn't taking me home? Allan just waited with me in silence; he said I should get something to eat and change into something dry. I couldn't brace myself to go into the house! He asked if I wanted to go to Janelle's, his sister, since she lived close by. I didn't answer so we drove to hers. Uncle Eddie and Aunty Elaine were upset I called so late but they understood I had forgotten I had plans with Janelle to sleep over and only remembered at the last minute. They still think Liam dropped me at hers...the one
and only time I lied to them.

What had taken place between Liam and I was the past now. I learned my lesson. I also realized that one can recognize true friends during hardships and trials. With every hardship in life, your so-called "friends" would go through 'a strainer': only the solid, real friends would stay. As my uncle would always say: 'A real friend is the one who walks in when the rest of the world walks out.'

Well, that would summarize my feelings about the situation with Liam. After what happened that night, Liam became more distant. I tried to discuss the incident and tell him how I felt. But that conversation was too deep for him. I'm not even sure if we can call it a conversation. Actually, I still can't figure out if Liam was seriously involved in our relationship. This was our first hardship. If we felt serious about each other we should have been able to overcome it as love conquers all things. Liam was probably not ready. I was more serious about us than he expected, I wasn't just in for the fun. But I was also hopeful for the future, still looking forward to build a strong trust with Liam despite this incident. After all we were still young and nobody is perfect. That was then.

Sadly, with time we became distant.

I've never been a suspicious or jealous person. I decided to block my ears to gossips about my boyfriend Liam in order to protect my inner peace. Thinking about all the sacrifices I endured in this relationship, I felt betrayed. With time and being busy with other activities, I found the strength to let it go. As time went by, Liam and I stopped talking. Actually I stopped trying to reach him. My relationship with Liam was an emotional roller coaster, a situation the person I am now would have handled differently.

We never really broke up, never had a conversation to sort things out…No closure. I've heard people say that 'closure' is a woman thing. I think everyone would like to know why a relationship didn't work so you don't repeat the same mistakes over and over again!

Liam stopped calling. At first, I didn't care… well I was convincing myself I didn't. Then I kept leaving messages, checking his Facebook page to see where he was, what he was doing! I drove several times by his house and called him from his parking lot with no success!

My aunty and uncle knew Liam's parents. They were friends. For the sake of that friendship, I never really told them what happened between Liam and I. For my family, my relationship with Liam was viewed as 'young love.' This love was intense but fragile. My uncle once told me: "we all want to be loved but not everyone is truly ready for it. You just need to be patient."

I knew my aunty was actually relieved. She thought we were too young to handle anything serious. As for my best friend Allan, he said I was 'just stupid for a moment'. Allan never really liked Liam due to the fact that I was so deep in love with him. Allan said I trusted Liam blindly when I shouldn't have because he clearly didn't deserve it.

I thought that's what true love was supposed to be.

I guess I've learned the hard way! You can't give your whole heart and soul too soon. But when do you know it's the right time to trust a person completely? And if you always hold back, how would the person know it is ok to trust you in return?

I had never been good at math and for me, love felt like one big equation to solve.

Anyway, Allan, had always been there for me, especially in those moments when I was about to lose my mind. I remember the day he gave me a ride to Liam's place, another one! It was the last time...

The day before we left for Europe. Everyone thought it was finally over with Liam! I was so into our project, from convincing my uncle to making all the bookings and other plans. My aunty was happy to help me pack, saying how proud she was to see me explore different horizons. But something strange took place the day before our flight and I felt the need to see him again. I told Allan I was going to go by Liam's one last time but he insisted on giving me a ride. I wasn't emotionally prepared to go there alone he said. I was so convinced that he would open the door. But I was once again very disappointed…

Our trip to Europe was such a relief; it was a well-deserved time off of all this drama! When we got back from Europe, I thought I would start afresh, put the past behind me. Today that past resurfaced just when I was ready to move forward with my love life. How can I make a wise decision?

The meeting with French Connection went well. They loved Allan's design and had accepted all our clauses in the contract. They asked me to team up with one of their experts in order to direct the photoshoot. Discussions took place regarding an Ad or billboard.

Thousands of ideas were already fusing in my head and I still couldn't believe all the great things that were happening to me, to us.

My phone vibrated again, a reminder to check my books in at the library! And a reminder that a text message from Liam was still unanswered!

To the end of the road

I was on my way to the UCLA library. There was an exciting reality about driving through Los Angeles at night. The busy streets, the multiple sounds and chatting echoing like one single melody; the odds that are so prevalent that the casual pedestrian eventually becomes the real odd one. I usually prefer it when someone else is driving. I would sit back on the passenger seat and imagine what my life would be like if at that moment I was one of those pedestrians walking down Westwood Boulevard. Sometimes it made me feel happy other times I would feel depressed, it's very strange.

As I was parking my car, my phone started ringing. I picked it up without looking at the caller ID.

"Hello princess! What are you up to?"

"Liam?"

I knew I should have checked the caller ID.

I was not ready to talk to him now. I really didn't know what to say, I didn't want to get back into the person I used to be. This naive girl who was so much in love she would believe just anything.

To be honest, I was still this girl because I had never got mad at him!

I even forgave him without him asking. I only managed to scream and get mad at him in my imagination. I played the scene in my mind: I would drive to Liam's place and as soon as he opens the door give him a piece of my mind and drove off! Only in the real world, I had never had the courage to do that. It was not in my DNA to act like that. Never mind, I was a strong woman now, I could handle anything now...I think.

"Hey Liam." I answered .Stuttering. "I'm just checking my books in at the library!"

"Really? I live nearby, you know that."

"I know."

"Did you receive my text? Alex is taking some homies hiking this Saturday afternoon. Want to join?"

"I'm not sure…"

"It's going to be a real reunion with old friends I'm sure you'll love it!!! Listen Ajia, now that you back in LA I would love to see you! I still want us to talk…"

"I'm not sure…"

"I understand. I think there is no better setting than a relaxed environment to talk, Ajia. I know Santa Monica is your favorite place."

"Yes, I do love Santa Monica."

"I knew it!! We will go to the Getty View trail! You will enjoy taking amazing pictures there! You do know the Getty View trail is the best hiking spot in LA!!!!"

"Wow, since you got all my soft spots covered! We've never been to the Getty view trail before… Can I bring a friend?"

"Alex insisted on having a small group and to be honest, I really want it to be just us."

"I thought this was a group activity."

"It is, with a couple of friends we both know. What I really want to say is …I'm done making excuses and running away from my fear. I really hope this is the right time to talk to you, Ajia!!"

My heart started beating out of my chest, Liam was finally being honest about his shortcomings and yet I was nervous as to what was coming. By the way, what was coming?

"Alright, text me the details."

"Is that a Yes?"

"It's a: 'I'll think about it and let you know ASAP'. Speak to you later Liam."

Saturday came by really fast. Our mutual friend, Alex, who was organizing the hike on the Getty View trail, phoned me to personally invite me. He said it would be nice to catch up; although we used to hang out a lot when Liam and I were still dating Alex was among the many friends I lost touch with after Liam walked out of my life so yeah It would be nice to catch up, he's a nice guy. I suspected that Liam might have been behind it but I accepted Alex's invitation and texted Liam to confirm the plan. Alex was very independent and busy in his architectural projects. I'd never seen him interfere in his friends' relationship before. He was the type of person who enjoyed life drama-free. We all met at Alex's place near Bel Air. From there, we all went in his car, big enough to fit the six of us: Alex, his cousin Tamara along with her best friend Lucy, Tamara's fiancé Genesis, Liam and I. I knew Tamara from high school as she also grew up in Long Beach. She was filling me in on her recent engagement and how she met Genesis. As we drove to the Getty Centre area, we soon found the Getty View trailhead on Sepulveda right by the 405 overpass. The view was amazing, and I was already taking pictures. The houses were very impressive and beautiful. I just wished it wasn't so smoggy; otherwise the view of the city and possibly the Pacific would have been very nice as well. Alex parked and paid the 8$ parking fee.

"Ok guys. I hope you have enough water. I have some in this cooler, please help yourself. Don't forget to put enough sunscreen because this trail doesn't have a lot shade areas. Yes, even black people need sunscreen lotion. The trail is about 6 miles out and back so it would probably take us about 2 hours max."

Alex continued.

"The elevation is only 600ft so Ajia you should be alright! I took a blue inhaler just in case."

"Thank you, Liam. I should be alright with mine, but I appreciate the attention."

"Alright guys, let's go!" Alex said, as he took the lead toward the hiking path.

After the walk, the run

Liam was right; hanging out with old friends was so much fun! And rekindling with Los Angeles' natural scene even better. I have to say I haven't been hiking since I got back from Europe, I didn't realize until now how much I've missed this landscape. The heat was a little difficult to handle but with plenty of water, we were able to stay hydrated. The girls in our group often got into deep conversations. It's not that I wasn't interested but I really wanted to enjoy our God-given wonderful creation and meditate on it. I felt so happy and content in this natural beauty.

What a blessing!

I enjoyed the hiking and seeing my favorite flower everywhere, the bird of paradise. Only an intelligent and considerate Creator would have made such wonder for humans to enjoy. After all why are there so many species of flowers? Varieties of trees? Colors? Isn't for the purpose of enjoying their beauty? It's just amazing. Every time I'm exposed to nature, I'm left in awe.

 The girls were still conversing, far behind us .So, the rest of us decided to wait for them. Right at that moment, we noticed something crossing our path. I couldn't tell what it was exactly but just as Tamara was about to take a step forward, the creature was slowly crawling and making its way to the opposite side of the road.

It was a rattlesnake.

I was impressed by the way the girls handled themselves. They didn't scream, nor did they panic! They just quietly stepped away from that snake!

I don't think I would have handled it so well. For me, seeing a rattlesnake is always a nerve-wracking moment. Even though we had a good laugh once everyone was safe, we were all conscious of how serious this could have been.

When we reached the top, we took a break to admire the view: a beautiful 360-degree view of the entire Los Angeles Landscape .We sat there for half an hour and it felt so good. It was quiet and I felt refreshed .Quite the opposite of the rush and noise of the city. I should really get back to hiking more regularly.

On our way back to the car, Alex offered to have us all back to his place and enjoy the pool. We thought it was a great idea. Once we reached Alex's house, Liam asked me if we could take a walk to 'talk.'

I agreed but only if I could take a shower first and change. I was trying to gather my thoughts as the water ran through my body, but I couldn't. What was I going to say to this man? Did I need to say anything? I was so fed up about the whole situation with Liam...

I really feel like I no longer have time for that drama …

Maybe I could just sneak out and let him hang like he did to me so many times. I could call an Uber and ask him to wait down the road, then walk out through the back door. If anyone saw me, I could just make up an excuse... Would that be too mean? I didn't know… I already agreed to meet with him, so let's just do it.

 "You alright? Liam asked."

"I'm ok."

"Well Ji, I mean Ajia. First, thank you for being here and being you. If you have something in your mind and would like to tell me, I'm ready to hear it."

I was in shock, but wait why would I be? Being a nice person sometimes made me forget that some people just cannot mature fast enough. Why would I think Liam had changed just because he was back at his sweet smiles and thoughtful attention?

"Please tell me this is a joke!" I said a little bit upset. "Are you going to tell me what you invited me here for? You are holding the cards, Liam. Either you talk or I'm out."

"Don't get upset. All I'm saying is I haven't been listening to you. I mean we've been through a lot these past few years and I know there is no excuse for how I behaved, Ajia. I am truly trying to change! Ajia, please don't give up on me!"

Looking at him in the eyes, I couldn't say a word. He continued:

"I'm happy to see that you are still the beautiful, kind person I knew, and I love you for that. I received the emails you sent from Europe. At that time, I was too deep in my own mess to mind communicating to friends and loved ones. And I regret it. I'm trying to put things back together in my life. I realize now that I wasn't paying attention to what you were saying. I didn't take care of you the way a man is supposed to take care of a woman he loves!"

"That is...very kind .We were not married so you never had such responsibilities towards me. Now I'm a bit confused as to what exactly your point is ...I have the feeling you only take matters seriously when it touches your self-esteem. You disappeared from my life for over a year! I don't know what to say…"

"I really messed up, I take full responsibility for it and…"

"Actually," I said interrupting him, "I know exactly what to say: You did hurt my feelings Liam. Really bad! I felt angry for a while but now I'm just confused. I'm not sure I want to re-visit that."

"Can you forgive me Ajia? Like I said I know I really messed up! You are the only one who really believed in me. I couldn't see it and maybe I wasn't mature enough to handle the situation right. I promise you, I am a new person, at least I am really trying to be this time. Please forgive me, babe."

"I'm still confused, Liam."

"I understand. I'm so sorry for the pain I've caused you! Will it be possible to start over?"

In moments like this, I definitely wish my life was a movie so I could pause and call Allan for his input.

In many situations where I disagreed with him, I still valued his unbiased opinion. Plus his input had kept me out of trouble. Allan has been my 'voice of reason' when my mind couldn't deal with my emotions!

"I will…I mean I forgive you. There is no point to hold on to the past. But it can't just go back to being the same. We can try to be friends again. I need time to rebuild trust, I want to believe you've changed really but I need to actually see that to be convinced."

"Fair enough. I believe in us. You're holding me at a distance but I've never felt so close to you. I will do my best to win you back. I know you still have feelings too. I can feel it."

I started to feel cornered, but I wasn't going to let him play with my feelings again! The frightening thing was that I still loved him. I was also over being told what my feelings should be. In the past, I was so scared of being left out that I allowed others to dictate my feelings. I had always tried to please others so they wouldn't leave me.

I was so wrong!

I had changed now and I was determined to keep control of my life. So yes, I still loved Liam, but I had the power to control my feelings. I understood now that being in love didn't automatically make the relationship healthy. I really needed time and space to figure this out. My silent prayer was answered when I noticed a voice message on my cell. It was from my best friend Allan.

"I'll think about what you just said. To be honest, I need time. I need to go. I have an emergency", I said pointing at my phone, "I'll talk to you later, Liam!"

"Alright, I understand. I will call you; there is that restaurant I would love to take you to, the cuisine is just out of this world, Ajia! Please let me, Ok?"

"Maybe."

"Bye babe."

Liam hugged me so tight, I felt uncomfortable for a minute. I couldn't help but think: "what if Anthony saw us?" Here we go, that was truly a feminine thought. I just met the man and yet I was already loyal to him. Acting like we were already dating when we were barely getting to know each other. It was silly although funny. I don't think a man would think like that. Unless you clearly say 'let's date officially', for a man you are just friends. Men can hold your hand, pay for your dinner, take you out on a date, have long conversations on the phone, yet still view you as 'just a friend' unless you had that crucial conversation. I don't want to say all men are like that but I'm just talking from what I've seen and experienced.

As a woman, I naturally studied with care any relationship that I have with the opposite sex. People would say: "She's already planning the wedding!" Well, not exactly, but we do need to make plans. I believe that when it comes to dating, women need to set their guards around their heart even when exploring new possibilities. That's the only way not to get hurt!!

I ran back to the house to get my bag then I called an Uber even if Liam offered to drive me back.

Cleaning the tank

The Uber was driving me to Allan's place. What had just happened? I tried to process in mind every details of my conversation with Liam. As soon as Allan saw my face, he knew something was wrong. We were now sitting in the summer garden drinking soft drinks. I tried my best to narrate exactly what had happened. I didn't want to leave out any details.

"So I send you a text about how I got a new fish tank and you ran? Hilarious!"

"I needed an exit. You know I don't do so well under pressure. Besides, you said you might need my help to set it up!"

"Yeah here is the tank and all these pieces to put together… it's a bit more work than I anticipated. You ARE the worst under pressure. I'm glad you came, I really hope you are not planning to get back with him, Ajia!" Allan said, shaking his head.

"What, you don't approve?"

"No, I don't, even if it's not my place to approve or not. I do not trust him and I don't believe he won't hurt you again. Are you considering it? Don't answer! I'm already upset. And please don't give me that puppy look… Don't cry now Ji! You deserve better, don't let him take too much of your space and energy."

"I know…It's not in my nature to judge people so I can't say if he's being truthful or lying again. One thing I can tell you is, I've already forgiven him. I can no longer hold grudges, Allan! That's what's eating up my energy."

"I understand, Ajia…"

"Where are you going to put this gigantic tank? And please tell me it's for fish and not another snake."

"You will see it soon! So, what are you going to do about Liam?"

"I'm going to take it one day at a time. I'm going to: do me. Like you always say. I will enjoy my return to California, get that degree and get our business on the way. Whatever happens in between won't change that."

"That's my girl."

Cleaning and setting up Allan's new aquarium was quite relaxing after all. The tank was very big; it actually lightened up the living room, giving it a whole new feeling. We sat there for a while and stared at the clear water. We pictured in our mind how beautiful fishes would be swimming through the decor we had just put in.

"You should get baby sharks, it's big enough. Do they have dwarf ones?"

"Dwarf!? Ha-ha you such a dork!"

"I mean miniature species of shark...Look how clear and simple this aquarium is...I need to do some cleaning in my life too."

"Yes, but that's life dear. And we're humans, not fish or any other kind of animal. Messy situations and issues are part of our trip. You just go through it and learn from it. The key is to try not to repeat the same mistakes while moving forward, we are constantly moving forward just like time."

"I hear you. I have to admit I am quite excited about what's ahead for me, but I am scared to make the wrong choices and step back in my old stupid ways."

"It's called growing up. Sometimes you have to step back to better jump forward. And your ways are not stupid! Now come over here. I'll show you what goes in the aquarium and don't you scream now!" Allan added with a big smile on his face.

Flashback

Three days had gone by, and I was quite busy working an assignment due soon. Right after submitting the assignment, I realized I had not heard from Liam since the hiking trip. Not that I was expecting anything special about him. I already knew that when he will show up again, he will certainly say something like "I figured you needed space to think." I did need time and space though. And part of me was wishing he would just forget about me forever. Ok, I had admitted only a few days ago still loving him. I was not denying it today. It's just that despite those feelings, I was not the same person I used to be when we were together. I had left her, the 'old me', back at LAX airport a year ago. Let me take you back:

"Allan, how would I just leave the country and not meet him once more? And for a whole year!"
"Ajia please don't start again! We've been through that yesterday. And although I wasn't happy about it at all, we called him ten times. We even drove all the way to Huntington to see if he was home, but he wasn't there! His family knows you've tried to reach him so they must have told him, and still he didn't get back to you. So drop it now. Let it go!"
"I know, you probably think I'm being silly right now. I think I've hurt him by turning my back on him! Maybe that's the reason why he's reacting this way. But if I could just…"
"Correction, you didn't turn you back on him. You learned the truth about him, tried to fix it but it didn't work. So you decided to focus on yourself. Don't feel bad about it, Ajia. Ok, don't cry now."
"Oh… I'm not crying"

"Soon we'll be on that plane to Paris. You've made it Jia, you've dreamed about this trip and you've made it come true. Don't cry, he's not worth it!"

I remember that moment when I stepped into the plane, anxious about this new chapter in my life. In addition to my anxieties, the fear of flying wasn't helping. Allan was seating next to me and was taking out his iPod, magazines, and other entertaining items from his backpack. I was just staring at my phone, eyes filled with tears, hoping it might ring before the flight attendant asked me to turn it off. I was hoping he would call me back, just to hear his voice one more time. That never happened and for the next 12 hours flight every time I felt asleep I would have these vivid flashbacks of our firsts. First kiss, first date, first love:

Liam and I have had common friends for years. We never really hung out together until the night his dad threw a housewarming party. That night, we talked about various topics but mostly art, which we were both very interested in at the time. We had an intense and deep conversation. I could barely hear the music anymore, just his voice and mine… The week that followed, I was driving when I got a phone call.

"Hey girl! It's Liam. How you been?"

"Not too bad. What about you?"

"I'm good. I haven't seen you since the party, well besides the pictures my dad took. I didn't even get to share them with you."

"Oh wow hope I don't look too bad! To tell you the truth I didn't know you wanted to talk to me. It's not like we usually hang out, I don't know."

"You kidding! I gave you my number after all. You are just being shy. I should be the one impressed by such a smart and beautiful young woman like you. Listen, I'm going hiking with some friends this Friday. You remember Alex, from Bel Air? I would love it if you join us and…err…there is this nice burger joint I was thinking we could go to in the evening."

"Hmm, I've never been hiking you know…Well, that could be interesting and then we are all going for a bite?

"I was thinking just you and I for a dinner date… Or maybe a double date if you prefer."

I had never really been on a date before, but the chat we'd had at his dad's party was so nice that I was confident I would have a great time with him. He seemed like a really nice guy. Of course, uncle wanted to have the "chat" with him when he came to pick me up! Fortunately, it wasn't too embarrassing. Liam had a way with my uncle, they became really close with time.

My first-time hiking was amazing; Alex and the other friends were so funny! We drove down to Malibu, ocean on the left, mountains on the right. I was sitting in the front right by Liam who was driving and talking to me at the same time. I felt like a princess. He had arranged water, a fresh towel, some fruits, and other snacks for me. He offered to carry everything so I wouldn't hurt my back.

I was mesmerized by the view from up the hills but also by this caring guy. His manners, the way he spoke to me…I was beginning to fall for him. As we drove back home, Liam started to tell me about the restaurant and how he would pick me up at 8 pm.

That's when friends in the car started teasing him about them being hungry too. We all laughed but they were serious. As he walked me to my door, he hugged me and asked if it was ok if his friends came along this evening as they would surely not give up. I had no problem with them. We all had so much fun together and to be honest, I was feeling a little apprehensive about a one-on-one evening with him. Or was it because I left the 'just the two of us' aside when I told Uncle Eddie about our dinner arrangement?

Dinner went very well. We had a good laugh playing silly games like 'truth and dare' while waiting for desserts. When the bill arrived, Alex and Liam fought over it to pay. Then Alex left with other friends while Liam and I were walking to his car: a black Mercedes with a Louis Vuitton interior.

I had already teased him about this 'showy display of one's means of life.' He told me that he didn't really like it, but his dad had picked the interior; the car was a graduation gift. I was about to comment on it when a chill ran down my spine: Liam was holding my hand…

All of a sudden everything went dark. When I opened my eyes, Allan was staring at me, worried. No wonder, I was squeezing his arm so tight that it left marks.

"Sorry I was dreaming…well, more like a flashback. It was real; I mean exactly how things had happened…"

"Are you ok? Don't worry we are landing in about half an hour. Here try these cookies or as French people call it: 'biscuit.'

While we were waiting for our luggage at the CDG airport, in Paris, I made a silent prayer. I promised I was done crying. This was a new opportunity, so I needed to be selfish for a minute and enjoy it fully. The next day Allan wanted to try an authentic French barbershop that we had spotted while walking to our apartment. As he got his hair cut, I decided that I would completely change my look, to reflect this new chapter in my life. I had the barber cut my hair short, bald short. I felt so happy and liberated! It's funny how hair, especially for black woman, could hold so much meaning. It could be burdensome sometimes. That extra pressure because people would judge you through your hair so you try and keep you hair a certain way, straight, tamed, sleek to fit in and be taken seriously. So yeah, it felt very liberating not to have them anymore. At first I felt like I was doing something I was not supposed to do, I almost called Aunty Elaine to apologize! Then I felt naked so for the first few days I wore hats and scarfs. And finally I had no choice but to own it. Yes the focus was now on my face; the shape of my skull, every single twitch and emotion were exposed. Over the first weeks in France, I had grown to love this new me and was ready to show the world who I was deep inside. Throughout my stay I was gaining more confidence in myself, I was finally ready to move on from Liam not only physically but emotionally too!

This flashback was long but I really needed to share this with you so you could get the full picture of my history with Liam. You could see now why I was feeling torn, like I was at a crossroad: exploring a possible new chapter with Anthony or giving Liam a second chance.

24 Hours

"How did your exam go?" Anthony had asked me to join him at the 24-hour gym. I was on my way to my own gym when he called to check on me. He already had a proper workout before I arrived so he offered to coach me. Lately Anthony had taken the habit of checking on me regularly. He always texted or called me after class.

"It went very well thanks. Even though it wasn't the actual exam yet, it was just a preparation quiz."

"Ok, it's always good to be prepared. Alright, should we try this machine now? Have you tried it before? It's quite easy."

"Is that so? It looks pretty difficult to me. I have no muscles on those arms!"

"Come on I'm sure you do! Let me show you: you actually have this support here at the bottom to help you. I would use it to get you started and once you've warmed up you can try without..."

I enjoyed working out with Anthony, although that boy made me work hard! He was so patient and explained everything so carefully. When I went to play basketball with his cousins two days ago, Anthony stayed on the bench watching us.

"It was nice hanging out at the court the other day. I'm curious tough, why don't you play Basketball?

"You mean: how come a black man doesn't play basketball? Isn't that cliché Miss Ajia?"

"I know but I actually meant have you stopped playing for a particular reason or you just don't like the game. I mean most of your family play!"

"Yeah I know. I don't know, I'm just not cut out for it. I suppose I don't enjoy it as much as other sports like tennis or running. I do enjoy watching a good game though."

"Lakers fan?"

"No, but I won't say it out loud in a public place like this one."

"Fair enough. I've never asked: in which field do you work?

"I'm glad you never asked because it's boring. I'm a management consultant. See, nothing fancy but it gives me the freedom to be my own boss. I get to choose who I want to work with and when I want to work....well I do have deadlines though."

"Very interesting, really! I think being your own boss is amazing. Plus you don't have to deal with office gossip."

"And you, what are your plans? You seem to work so hard at law school and yet your energy is split with photography. Do you plan on picking one in the future?"

"Do I have to? I meant I've pursued law at first because my uncle wanted me too, and in the end I love it. The idea that you can make someone's life better, help them solve their problems, is very exciting!"

"I agree. Ajia!"

"As for photography, it is a passion. Something I can do whenever I feel like it! Photography gives me a way to freely express my creativity without the pressure of a client who just wants to put out content that sells his product and connect with people's pocket rather than their mind."

"Was Allan a good client? I saw your feature online."

"It's out already? No, Allan is not a client. He's my best friend and business partner. We've created this brand together. I'm happy we are getting some good exposure already."

"Wow, that's quite an accomplishment Ajia. Will you have time for anything else? Your life seems so full already. "

"Anything else? Like what?"

"Like a family."

"I do have one! And don't worry, I spend plenty of time with them. I have to remind myself to be balanced sometimes but overall I do well."

"I mean you own family, a husband, and child maybe children."

"Oh, I feel so silly! That kind of family!" I said laughing.

"Would you like to have kids someday?" Anthony asked again.

"I don't know. I haven't thought that far yet, to be honest. It's something I'll have to discuss with the man I'll fall in love with. You know my future husband."

"Fair enough! I would love to tell my future wife that I see us having two beautiful children, twins!"

"What?! Twins? I'd like to see that..."

"Guys! We've been here for hours! Should we get some frozen yoghurt? I am starving!" Carlton said, coming out of nowhere.

"Come on man, you just got here. Plus you said you wanted to enroll." Anthony replied to Carlton, teasing him.

"That will be for my next visit, I can't do anything with an empty stomach," he said touching his belly.

"Where have you been anyway? Did you even work out?" I asked Carlton.

 I had not even noticed Carlton had disappeared a while ago.

"Of course I did. More than you actually," he said staring at both of us with a suspicious look on his face. I saw an interesting class near the changing room as I was walking out! They were biking underwater; it looked so cool!! I went and had a go. Now I'm dead tired and hungry. Let's go eat!" He said, walking away.

"I apologize for my cousin's rudeness."

"It's ok Ajia. He's right .we've worked out enough I'm a bit hungry too. Besides, we can carry our conversation in a quieter place!"

"Frozen yoghurt, here we come!" my cousin said, leading the way while I was looking at the back of his head, ready to smack it if he put me through further embarrassment.

Spiritual Feast

As I walked down the road,
I saw my man
Coming from the Earth he was
He emerged from the ground,
His broad shoulder pushing out the asphalt,
I watched
I felt attracted to his presence, a manifestation
Of the prince the little girl in me still believed in
I raised my arm to reach him but fell upon my knees
Trembling
Gripping the grass I closed my eyes in prayer
I raised my head to look again, he was still there
Standing, his body fully off the ground
His eyes locked in mine as he delivered his message
In silence
His words touched my ears as he told me how
At the beginning of humanity, when he was being molded
He had been blessed with God's wonderful attributes
That in His image he was made to praise and testify for His
wisdom
He explained how with his rib I was made to join him and be-
come
One
He cried as he showed me how throughout history
Women led themselves away from their head
That we pray for a spiritual man to come
But couldn't see him with our heads unveiled
He showed me how men oppressed the weaker vessel
How they made us believe we were weak in mind and spirit
Earth drifting from the order God cherished

But we ARE the most precious creation, equal to man
Yet submitted
I watched and listened in awe,
I understood there was hope, for humans
Had in them to imitate Godly qualities
I watched as he leaned closer to me
He took my hand and whispered in my ear:
'God loves a spiritual woman, it's the only woman he would
draw close to'

My alarm clock screamed painfully in my ears. I felt like I had not slept at all and this was bad. I rushed to the bathroom to check the damage on my face, only to find my cousin had already beaten me to it. His singing made my pounding head even worst. I walked down to the kitchen. My aunt was already up actively sorting out our lunch packs while listening to music. It felt so nice, the smell of fresh coffee and hot muffins. I loved going to these conventions! It usually lasted Friday through Sunday and it was a very up building moment for my family as well as friends sharing our faith.

Today was the first day of this yearly event. I was planning to wear this fabulous African dress; I absolutely love the modern pattern mixed with a very traditional fabric. I used a matching piece to wrap my hair in a pineapple afro. I chose some wooden drop link earrings and a simple gold chain necklace to match the outfit.

I felt butterflies in my stomach at the thought that Anthony will be there. I had to finish up with my makeup, as time was running out. I laid all my brushes on the countertop, trying to remember my friend's Viola's tutorial. First, I should start with the eyebrows and then the eyes before finishing with the foundation. Once I finished up my makeup, I did a last check-up at my bag to see if I had everything. We finally reached the convention center. Uncle Eddie lectured us about the virtue of being 'on time at God's table.' My cousin Carlton was nodding his head in approval from time to time, especially when my uncle was taking a look in the rearview mirror. I could see his small headphones pressed in his ears. The volume was not too loud, to allow him to follow the conversation or rather the monologue.

We arrived an hour early although it was 5 minutes late on my uncle' own schedule. The center was getting filled with friends as I spotted Jannell and her husband. After a brief catch up, I joined her brother, Allan, by the stage to help him practice his interview. I had not seen Anthony yet. He had texted me yesterday about being excited to see me today though. Allan, a bit more confident, went backstage and I left to find my seat. I met some friends on the way most of whom I had not seen in a while. One of them, Michel'le, was about to take a group picture, when Liam showed up, right next to her. He offered to take the picture so Michel'le could get in the picture with the rest of us. My stomach tightened a bit, just a nervous reaction I couldn't control. Liam smiled and winked at me. How arrogant!

I wasn't upset at all. I couldn't, there was absolutely no reason for me to be upset. Well, ok I was a little but I smiled back. But just then, I spotted Anthony right behind him. Now I started to feel sick, and I'm sure my face read panic all over. I was anxious some kind of drama would happen such as Liam walking up and giving me his unique greeting hug, after which he usually touches my chin, while Anthony would watch the whole scene and stomp towards him with a 'stay away from my girl' frown on his face ready to launch at Liam...ok more realistic? Anthony would watch the whole scene, turn around and walk out assuming I was still seeing someone. I never told him about Liam, well I did talk about someone breaking my heart to pieces when we confided each other's past love stories and he was pretty upset about it so my first theory was not so unrealistic. Anyway, my nerves soon had a rest when Anthony walked away toward the exit looking at his phone.

He had not seen us.

"Hello, gorgeous!"

"Hi, Liam! I didn't expect to see you here."

"Well, I thought I'll come and catch up with everyone. Besides your uncle told me you guys would be here."

Uncle Eddie? Really? I'm going to have a serious talk with him about putting his nose into my business, not like we had not already had that conversation a thousand times! Last week, he was telling me, on our way to the dentist, how easy it is to start a fire when the embers were still hot. I pondered on it the whole ride trying to figure out the connection with my dentist appointment. Now I understood and I was not happy about it.

"Are your parents here? I haven't seen Aunty Faye in a long time!"

"I'm afraid not! They went on a cruise for their anniversary. Where are you sitting?"

"That's sweet! I'm sitting right there on the balcony. I guess I see you around."

I left before he could reply. At that moment, I checked the time on my phone and realized I had a text.

"Morning! I was in the main hall looking for you, but the session is about to start. Hope to see you later, I'm seating on the balcony. –Anthony"

The day went by smoother than it started. We listened to some wonderful talks and Allan did a great job on his interview. He didn't seem too nervous at all. Later, we had lunch outside with my family and some friends! The Acton and the Johnson families were present as well. They are so sweet, and

I can understand why they would get along so well with my uncle and aunty. They have a very strong sense of family; in fact, they seem to have a lot in common! Actually, Anthony's dad invited us to a camping trip next weekend. I was staring at Anthony trying to figure out if he had anything to do with it but he didn't seem to be aware his dad was going to invite us. He seemed pleased though. When he took the coolers to the car I offered to help him out, I guess I was hoping to ask him if his family knew we were 'talking' to each other…but I felt embarrassed and didn't say anything. After all, were we really 'talking to each other'? Of course, my uncle was more than happy to accept the invitation. He had always loved camping trips but so far Aunty Elaine and I had always been able to avoid them. We've always preferred the comfort of a house or a hotel room for holidays: far more appealing! Anyway, they all seemed so excited about it and Kay Acton, Anthony' sister was assuring me that it was not as bad as it seemed. Now Kay was the definition of high maintenance so if I was going to trust someone regarding camping, it would be Kay! At the end of Sunday, the last day of this yearly convention, Aunty Judeline invited my family over for dinner. Aunty Judeline was Liam's great-aunt. You could never say no to her and to be honest, I was looking forward to her Haitian cuisine. Carlton and I had planned to meet up with friends after the convention but we promised to join the family at her house later in the evening. Aunty Judeline was a very sweet old lady, the oldest I knew. I've always loved visiting her and listening to her wealth of life experience while stuffing myself with her amazing food, Aunty Judeline could cook!! As for Liam, he felt quite the opposite and didn't really like visiting her because he would always get lectured. I didn't really understand what she was saying; I didn't speak a word of Creole. However from what Liam told me his family had very high, materialistic, expectations from him. It was somehow understandable because they had struggled to make it to the US and they didn't want the next generation, Liam's, to struggle too. He was supposed to have 'made it' in terms of career, wealth and family. But getting rich wasn't in Liam's agenda! Honestly, I admired him for that. He was very passionate about his art and didn't believe money or material guaranteed happiness. I remember one evening, Aunty Judeline had a party at her house. Liam's father got on his case, but my uncle diffused the tension with his famous jokes. Everybody went back to dancing, chatting and having fun when Liam left me in the crowded backyard to walk into the empty house. I waited for conversations to pick up and I followed him inside. I didn't want to raise any suspicion as very few of our folks knew we were dating. I was worried about him. This is the night we were planning to tell the rest of the family about our relationship! After trying to do so for weeks, it was yet another failure. It was dark so I tried to follow the dim light coming from the street light standing by the living room at the front of the house. After searching the living room to see if Liam was there I started to head toward the front door when someone caught my wrist and pull me down.

It was Liam sitting on the carpeted floor.

I was surprised to see him sitting in the dark. I asked if he was ok. He touched my chin and said he was happy I came tonight. Obviously not wanting to talk about what just happened, he took my hand and I could feel his stare in the dark.

I've dreamed about love, read about love, Watch it on TV, but I've never felt love like this before. Our faces touched, our nose…I could feel his breath and want. I closed my eyes. The room was dark but the electricity between us created a sparkle that would put to shame any Fourth of July firework. I wanted time to stop and us to stay there sitting on Aunty Judeline's floor forever; speaking with our eyes even though we couldn't really see each other in this dark room. Hours must have gone by. Either that or we had disappeared in a timeless dimension until Liam stood up and whispered: "We gotta go, baby." That was the first time he called me 'baby' and today I could clearly remember that feeling of belonging and longing that overtook me and didn't leave until…now.

Not long ago, thinking about my reaction to his sweet words made me both ashamed and angry at myself. How weak was I? Thinking he was mine? Because of what? Words? Touch? Those goosebumps I used to get whenever our skins grazed? But now I realize that it was true love, just that both of us didn't handle it the way it should have been. We were both too young with issues of our own maybe him more than me but I believe me too. This need to be loved…You would say I had my uncle and my aunt but at that time I was still angry with my dad, and not to feel that way I had to love unconditionally I guess.

Liam had this piercing stare; he would dive into my eyes and take control of my body. I remembered this painful and exciting jolt in my fingertips; sometimes I get it when I'm in a situation I shouldn't be in. That should have warned me if I knew my body that well back then. Yes, Liam and I sure had chemistry; we didn't have to talk most of the time to know what the other was thinking. I don't think that you learn that, to me, it just existed between two people or it didn't. Was that what a soulmate was? One to whom you would connect in that special way? I didn't really believe in soul mates though, this idea that we all had one matching soulmate somewhere in the world. If that were true we sure wouldn't fall in love so many times…

Anyway, I understand now, why Liam asked me if I had something to say. I avoided his eyes and got mad instead. But he wasn't speaking about words or whatever reproach I had. Liam could read me, read my hesitation, this longing that creeps back from time to time and that time was surely ill-timed. I went back down memory lane and my feelings had joined in for a moment.

But all of that belong to the past now.

I agreed to start over and be friends, just friends. We had a nice time hiking the other day and it felt great, like, when we were just friends. It reassured me that Liam and I could go back to that level and be ok even though he seemed to be on a different agenda for now. In my agenda, I was starting to fancy Anthony; I was still a little guarded but everything felt so simple with him. Even past the novelty of dating again, it was more the maturity of our exchange. Dealing, as a more mature woman, with a mature man. Anthony and I seemed to be on the same page in terms of understanding life goals and choices. He cared for what I had to say and how I was feeling about every single thing. Anthony would also make me laugh carelessly, not trying too hard but with a confidence that to me was even more attractive than anything else.

After the coffee, Anthony offered to drive Carlton and I to aunty Judeline on his way home. He had to finish some consulting work. It was sweet how he was trying to convince me to come to his family camping trip, obviously, he didn't know my uncle had already made that our official family summer trip. Which meant I was in the obligation to come anyway. He said it would be so much fun as his family loved me already (I think they are his secret weapon) and he enjoyed our company a lot.

 "No pressure just let me know. If you can't I'll understand."
"Ok, thank you for the lift. I'll keep you posted on that."

Pardon my French

Today was a very important day for Allan and me. We've worked so hard on our project which started as a 'let's try and do something to get him into fashion school' and had now become our baby. We have put all our passion and love for fashion and photography into that project and today we had the opportunity to present it to the public, more especially to fashion professionals. Well, it wasn't Milan fashion week, not even New York, but if this event goes well, we could get a shot at showcasing at London SS14.

After all, French connection had become one of the most talked-about brands at the London fashion show. I loved their innovative thinking. Who would have thought about releasing a special edition collection at each fashion week at an affordable price? I still had their bestselling "Wizard" dress in a limited-edition color for their 25th anniversary week. It only costed me about $30. The team that was put together for us today was truly amazing. They totally understood our viewpoint and Allan's direction for the brand.

Of course, it required many meetings and workshops, but the collaboration was smooth and enjoyable. The day had finally arrived to shoot our diffusion line; selected pictures would be featured in FCUSA stores as well as fashion magazines for promotion. Allan's designs were mesmerizing, without bias of course! Simplicity and purity that he certainly gained from his experience in Europe! Mixed with African colors and patterns. We made a point of bringing our 'roots' back to these modern times. The models we've chosen were very authentic.

We made sure we had a variety of shapes and shades; we did not hesitate to go for the darkest skin tones. This was my personal input, not because I was dark skin myself but there is such a raw beauty in darker skin! The venue was also a gem. There was a building in downtown LA that the city was planning to destroy next month. This Building was empty except for street artists; to allow them to display their works. It was so fascinating to see how they had transformed each apartment and room into a walk-in gallery. It was just perfect that we found it!

I didn't see the time go by except for a way too long lunch break. Allan's girlfriend showed up to surprise him with lunch. At first, he wasn't too happy because it kind of broke the vibe: we had decided to go over makeup and outfits arrangements for the afternoon session while the team and models took their lunch break. He eventually warmed up and I let both of them have their moment while I went to arrange my cameras.

As I was packing up my equipment at the end of the day, I started to think about the upcoming camping trip. I texted Anthony to tell him that we would love to come, and he seemed pretty excited. He said not to worry about equipment as they had everything. Anthony then asked if I'd be cool with sharing a tent with his sister Kay and he would share with Carlton.

Now, I feel some kind of way about that. My cousin's favorite subject was still about me even though he was older now and you would think he would have gotten over it. Plus, Carlton usually speaks in his sleep...

We agreed to all meet at Anthony's uncle's on Friday morning. He asked if I could ride with him, which I thought was really sweet. But I wasn't not sure my uncle would be too happy about that. Anyway, I was both excited and anxious about this whole trip. I've never been a camping lady, if such a term exists. I was scared of bugs, germs and how do you actually look decent on a campsite? Janelle, Allan's sister, promised to help me sort out outfits and necessities. We've made plans to go shopping tomorrow. Now I was driving to the hair shop to get some X-pression hair extensions. I had already planned my evening: box braiding while watching a movie. I will probably pick a Bollywood movie, first, because I really like them and then because they were usually so long it would keep me entertained during the whole braiding process. Actually, I would make it two movies: I was going to do medium size braids and my technique wasn't the quickest.

I should actually hurry up and get started.

Ready Campers

Shopping with Janelle was fun as always although we didn't get much camping related stuff! However, I got some precious big sister advice and cheeky tips on how to "get me a man", whatever she meant by it! Since Janelle got married, we haven't spent as much time together as we used to. Other than the fact that they moved further away from us, I think they were still in their honeymoon phase, enjoying each other and getting used to just be the two of them. I didn't blame her; she was doing 'her' just like she always told me to do: "Ajia, stop worrying about others, just do you, you are allowed to".

Janelle and Allan were like the siblings I've never had. We were closer than blood actually. We've spent most of our childhood together and I always looked up to Janelle, wanting to be like her. I loved the fact that although much older than Allan and I, she always included us into every "grown-up thing" she did. She was not ashamed to have us tag along when she hung out with her friends. And she didn't care about anything they said. Janelle never really cared about other people's opinion, I mean negative opinions or comments. She had always been a free-spirited person, so confident about herself. I wish I could say the same for myself but I was working on it.

Today was camping day! I was so excited I barely slept which is surprising since I didn't really like camping. Uncle Eddie was loading the truck with my cousin's help while Aunty Elaine was finishing up packing the third cooler, yes you read well: the third one. I started to wonder if they were planning on staying longer but again, I know aunty always planned meals like she intended to feed a nation! I was actually surprised at how much Carlton knew about camping: how to start a fire, raise a tent and so on. I was enjoying listening to him on our way to Anthony's parents. So far things were going well, maybe it will become a new hobby...if I survive the night in the wilderness.

When we arrived at the Acton's, both families were already there, some still loading the cars. After the usual greetings and jokes, we all split in different cars. Anthony was driving a black Escalade, his nephew Adam jumped at the back followed by Carlton. I hopped in the passenger side.

"Are you ready Miss Ajia?"

"I think so. Just to warn you, I might embarrass myself many times during this weekend but know that it's my first camping trip and I've given up getting along with spiders and bats a long time ago!"

"Ha ha, I got you. I will try my best to make this trip enjoyable for you. I promise. First, here is your oat milk iced mocha with caramel syrup! And I've packed all kind of snacks in the cooler at the back."

"Aww that is so sweet! Thank you. And wow! Look at this cooler! It's like a mini-fridge back there. By the way, I never seen this ride before."

"Yeah, I take this car out on special dates...I mean days. I've had it for a year now but I kept my old Chevrolet and somehow I'm using it more still."

"I guess it's cheaper on gas and easier to find parking in town with a smaller car rather than this big one. I like it though."

"You do? It's a decent ride, very comfortable for road trips. You know I was glad you guys decided to join us. It allows me to spend more time with you...which is something I've been wanting to do. Spend more time together, get to know each other. I don't want you to start feeling embarrassed and all but I've been giving a lot of thought about you...us."

"You are getting to know me well indeed! I am embarrassed. May I know what your thoughts were?"

"I guess we have the next couple of days to share them!"

"I can't believe I'm going to spend "days" in the wilderness! Not to sound spoiled but I've never done it no imagine doing that one day!"

"Ha ha, I like how you call camping 'wilderness'. Don't worry it's a national park and they have some basic facilities like showers, restrooms and so on. I also planned a little surprise that I'm sure you will love."

S'mores Traditions

We finally arrived at the campsite. The trip was quite long but we had a great conversation, sang along old school hits and played some games Carlton and Adam made up which made time really flew by. This place was quite impressive, those massive trees so tall as if they were trying to pierce the clouds. We parked in a clearing and had to walk a little through the trees to get to our camp spot. The floor was all dry dirt which was reassuring for me, it meant less bugs or at least I would be able to see them coming. But dirt also meant snakes so I wasn't sure anymore. Ok, I sound like a brat. I should relax and enjoy this beautiful landscape. I've been told this national park was quite big with great canyons and some wild animals. The men started on building up the tents; it sounded a little sexists when Uncle Johnson called out the guys to get on the task while the women get the food sorted but for once it did-n't faze me, especially when with well enough people on both tasks Anthony and I were left to fetch wood for the fire:

  "You really want to get the smallest ones. We should also get some leaves to help start the fire. The dry ones especially," said Anthony while showing me a piece of wood.
"Ok, like these ones? It's so refreshing to be here. The air re-ally feels purer than in LA!" I said.
"Yes, it really is a break from LA's heavy pollution especially at this time of the year. Escaping to nature is a must to survive city life."
"So, do you often get away like that Anthony?"
"I try to. I prefer more private settings though. Alone or with only one or two people but I do enjoy our family gatherings. There is a private beach I love to go to. It's so peaceful and quiet I used to pretend it was mine ha ha... I usually stay for

the weekend, hike, swim, do some fishing, just relax and enjoy God's beautiful creation."

"Where is it?" I said facing him.

"I can't tell you Ajia! But I will show you one day, it's paradisiac!"

"Alright now! Why can't you tell me? Are you afraid I'll steal your spot?"

"I'm afraid you would go without me or with someone else."

"Fair enough. Have you ever done it?"

"Done what?"

"Taken someone else? A friend I mean. "

"I've taken two of my friends but no girlfriend. I saw that smile."

"Pff right! I didn't mean..."

"That's ok Ajia. You know your eyes speak volumes. And I appreciate their honesty.

"Guilty! I didn't mean to be nosey, just curious. To be honest I've been waiting for you to mention why someone like you is still single. You are like the perfect guy...it is way too suspicious."

"You can ask me anything. Indeed, I rarely speak about my past, if not at all. I'm keener on looking forward than looking backward, you know. Plus, I am not as perfect as you think. Ajia!!!"

"None of us is. You have this thing...like a peaceful aura surrounding you. I'm talking nonsense but I mean any girl dreams to be with someone who makes her feel safe and appreciated, it's very attractive."

"Are you telling me that I am attractive, Ajia?"

"I'm saying you're a good guy Anthony."

"Ok. Well, thank you. And yet I am single, it's popular knowledge that girls prefer bad boys though! Anyway, you want to know a lot for someone who doesn't give much of her story."

"True. It's not a pleasant one. Quite complicated so I'd rather leave the book closed on that chapter."

"I hear you. I won't bring it up then. How about we start over and create new memories? Starting with an awesome bonfire and yummy s'mores."

"S'mores?"

"Don't tell me you don't know what s'mores are? It's the most amazing creation in the world of treats!"

"What does it taste like? What is it?"

"S'mores are traditional campfire treats. It's a roasted marshmallow and a layer of chocolate sandwiched between two pieces of graham crackers. You have to try, it's just the bomb!"

It was almost midnight, and nobody seemed to want to go to sleep. I have to admit that I was loving this camping business. We had a nice barbecue dinner and the s'mores were so tasty. Now, we were sitting by the fire, sharing jokes and family stories. I started to imagine what it would be to be with Anthony. Don't get me wrong I was not fantasying about Anthony. Just thinking about our current relationship and what it could lead to if I let my guard down. I was enjoying his company and seeing him with his family was even more attractive. I mean I love family dynamics; my family was so involved in my life I can't imagine settling with someone who wouldn't understand let alone accept it. Anthony's family was all up in his business! And I get it! This is the case with my family as well!

I would love to have a family tradition like that one day. Maybe we'll go camping with our grandchildren, have a bonfire at night and tell the story about how we fell for each other on my first camping trip. I was trippin'...

"I can get used to that." Now I tripped for real and jumped as Anthony whispered these words in my ear. Wasn't he just sitting opposite me? I could see his mouth open wide into a laugh then my eyes shifted to the flames from the fire, dancing high to consume the few marshmallows held at the end of thin sticks. And now he was kneeling next to me:

"You scared me! What did you say?"

"I said I can really get used to that. You and I by the fire...ha-ha sounds corny but it's true. Are you enjoying yourself?"

"Yes, I'm having a great time," I said.

"I'm glad to hear that! Will you be ok for the night? Your first camping night. We've done so much today I'm sure you'll sleep soundly until morning. I'm going to bed now. Lots of good things in perspective tomorrow."

Let's dive in

Jannell was so funny! I was laughing so much my stomach hurts. There are UNO cards everywhere looks like we made a mess when we were supposed to be working. Where exactly? Looked like an office with no front door. People were walking by, hi Tony! Nobody stopped except for him waving back but might be that we were paying more attention to our game and gossip than any business card that we apparently were supposed to hand out.

"Did you know Kerry and Ian split?" Seemed like I did know but somehow, I didn't say anything.

"Oh yeah?"

"Apparently, it went all the way left but I don't know what triggered it. One day she just erased all their pictures from Instagram..."

Janelle's voice sounded like some background music in a busy café.

I was so involved into the UNO game and laughing like crazy, I didn't know who we were playing with but they sure were funny.

"So, girls, how far did you get?"

Anthony?! All tuxedo up with a light pink bow tie?!

Oh, man! What a night. Did I even sleep? This crazy dream felt so real! I didn't like that. I was supposed to be well-rested and looking my best since I had minimal options to cover up the disaster of a restless night. Ok girl, relax! What was that dream by the way? Makes me smile though, it didn't make sense at all but Anthony was super cute! Anyway, I better get up and get to it instead of rambling on like a teenager.

"Here you go, mama."

"Oh, thank you, aunty!"

Aunty Elaine knows me best, I was not fully awake without my coffee. The cold shower by the campsite could have also done the trick or even laughing when Kay almost threw a tantrum when finding out there was nowhere to plug her blowdryer! I thought she was used to this camping thing! Anyway, the wash and go style suits her though, she'll be alright! I took my coffee and went for a walk. I had to go away for a minute just by myself, put my shades on like a proper LA girl, sip in my coffee like it was the last drink on earth and just be weird and in my zone. I would do that sometimes.

It's usually a car ride to wherever I need to be that day. Or a walk around our block and then I snap back. This was ten times better though, the quiet, the view, that smell untouched by urban soil. I was glad I took my camera! It was inspiring. Later on, we went on a hike, leaving the old folks behind (my aunty hated it when I called her old!). Anthony suggested we take our bathing suits, plenty of water and some snacks. We walked through the densest forest I had ever seen. The trees were so tall you would think they could reach the sky. Some of them were very thick! To think that some of these trees were thousand years old was mind blowing …

I was humbled.

It made me reflect on how important life was! We, as humans, don't get to live that long so each day should be celebrated and not wasted in useless fight or unproductive enterprise. I longed for the day we would live as long as those trees though. We then saw a herd of deers and just as I was trying to get closer, I saw a clearing then what looked like...water! It was so sudden, in the middle of this forest, we just came upon this wonderful spot. A waterfall was emerging with a pool at the base. The atmosphere suddenly became very tropical. We were so excited at this finding but Anthony seemed to know about this. We all stripped down to our swimming suits and jumped in the pool like some wild teen-agers, it felt amazing! The water was so refreshing.

After what seemed like hours leaping into the pool from one of the few high rocks surrounding the pool, I decided to take a break and chill on my towel.

 "Can I chill with you?" Anthony asked, water still dripping from his curly hair, down his body as he sat down next to me. I handed him a small towel.

"Of course. Thanks for bringing us here. It's really fun. Look at Carlton, he is having the time of his life! It's funny I re-member when we were teaching him how to swim, I thought he would never get it. Uncle Eddie and Aunty Elaine were very patient with him, and now he's jumping and doing som-ersaults into the pool!"

"Indeed he's got it now! You seem very close you two. You know at first, I thought he was your brother."

"Carlton IS like a brother to me! His dad is my mum's only brother. My biological dad was never in the picture, so Uncle Eddie really is my Father figure."

"I see, it's beautiful to see your guys' bond. If I may ask, have you ever met your dad?"

"I did but I barely remember him, I was just a baby. My par-ents met at University on the East coast. My dad was a foreign student and only after a month of meeting each other mum got pregnant. She didn't tell anyone from the family, and they tried to work it out and raise me while continuing with their studies…. but it was difficult."

I continued telling my story:

"When I was 2, mum visited Uncle and Aunty here in California that is when they found out I existed, and she told her big brother everything from the beginning. I don't know if my dad came with her and just didn't show up at my uncle's house. Anyway, she begged them to keep me for a while just the time for them to complete their studies and get a stable situation. Like I said my dad was a foreign student and his parents were financing his studies, he couldn't tell them about me yet, not until he was financially independent. Well that is what my mum told Uncle. So, I stayed here, mum would often call, send me letters and pictures of them both. She visited twice, the second time was when Carlton was born and then she never visited again.

I paused for a second to get hold of my emotion as I recounted that part of my life.

"As I was saying, my mom stopped writing to me, stopped calling. Uncle Eddie travelled to the East coast to see what was going on. When he got there, one of my mum's friends told him she had graduated and that they had attended my parent's wedding where they announced they were settling abroad. They didn't say where exactly. My mom 's friends also added that my parents were a very quiet and private couple. She believed that my parents had probably received a great job opportunity abroad because they were very smart."

"Oh wow, I had no idea Ajia," said Anthony while handing me a tissue.

"I guess they got their happy ending, but they forgot to get me back...Anyway, sorry I better stop talking, I am spoiling the day."

"Certainly not! It's your story, I am really sorry about that. It must have been difficult growing up and maybe now still."

"It was difficult but I have the most amazing family here, they filled every empty space I had with love and care and most of the time I don't even remember about my story. I focus on building good relationships and straightening them, well at least I try, I don't want my story to scar me if it makes sense. It's my parent's choice and I have my own choice: to pursue love and happiness no matter what."

"I feel you! Thank you for trusting me with your story. I hope to be another positive, happy and loving friend in your life. You really deserve it."

"That's very kind of you, Anthony."

"Before everyone rushes back, I'd like to ask you. Would you go on a date with me...I mean I'd like to take you on a date, we could go for dinner and then to a party in case you find me boring at least you would have enjoyed some dancing."

"You are definitely not boring. I would love to."

Take a bite

Today felt like the longest day of the year. I had three exams back to back. I was well prepared though; I had studied well with my group study and since coming back from camping I had not gone anywhere else except the library. Actually, I had studied so much that I had barely kept in touch with friends especially Anthony. He hasn't been tripping about it though, I guess he's not worried since we are going out on a date this Friday. Just as I was walking out the building, I could hear my stomach growling.

 "Girl, you need to put some food in that stomach!"

Gosh! That scared me! How rude, I mean...

"Liam? You scared me! I know. I haven't eaten since yesterday.

"You are still doing that? Forgetting to eat when you are very busy. How were your exams?"

"I suppose it went ok. How do you know about my exams?"

"I just guessed, why would you not eat all day if it were a normal school day? It's almost 5pm girl!"

"Yeah, I guess...what are you doing on campus?"

"I was looking for you. Let's go grab a bite, I know just the perfect place! Come on, I know you're hungry. Come on friend! See, boundaries," Liam said while starting to walk toward the parking lot.

I didn't really feel like hanging out right now even more with Liam, but I was so hungry plus he was being so silly right now it actually made me smile. I followed him to his car. We drove down Hilgard avenue when we took the ramp onto I-405 S, I asked where we were going, and he just said that I would love it. We finally pull out next to what looked like a typical street side taco. There was quite a long line. The aroma of delicious foods wafted through the sky. A man was making tortillas from a huge corn tortilla batter while a woman was putting meat on the grill to be cooked on what seemed to be mesquite.

Another man was putting the ingredients in the tacos like it was an art show and when he slammed the guacamole in my heart leapt, I felt like hugging Liam!

"One thing I remember clearly about you is how you love Mexican food. So, I present to you one of the best authentic Mexican street foods in LA."

"I have to say it looks good. I want to try one of every taco on this menu plus that mixto quesadilla. Should we get some beers?"

"Nah, I don't drink anymore but please have one!"

"That's new."

"I have changed a lot of things in my life. I had to and now I'm glad I was able to make amends with you. How about we try these goodies."

The food was delicious. We sat in a park close by. Liam took out a blanket for us to sit on as well as a small speaker. He wanted me to check out an artist he really liked at the moment: Omawumi. I absolutely loved it! Her voice was so powerful and yet soft. I was discovering new things about Liam, he has indeed made some changes and seemed more 'grown' than the Liam I used to know. It was actually nice to hang out with him and discuss his newfound love for Afrobeat, his new recording studio and all artists he was working with. I was really starting to appreciate him as a friend again and I loved that he wasn't trying to be more at the moment.

When the sun had set and it was getting too dark to hang out at this poorly lit park, Liam took me home. He didn't come upstairs just kissed me on my cheek and said we would catch up later. I was so tired I just crashed on my bed. My phone buzzed twice and I thought it was him texting me goodnight but it was actually a text from Anthony confirming our plan for Friday and giving me more details. I pulled myself out of bed to go shower and brush my teeth. I needed to clean up.

Peace out, A-Town

Friday night couldn't have come any sooner. I was so excited to go out with Anthony, to finally let myself fully vulnerable. I don't mean to do anything stupid but to really enjoy the date and the feelings that could arise; see if it was the beginning of something special. I felt ready, I was at peace with everything concerning Liam, and we had actually been texting each other as friends and it seemed like we were on the same page. Maybe I should have told him I was going out with Anthony but it really was not his business anymore. So tonight, was my big date with Anthony. I have to say I went all out. At first, I brought out my sexy black dress, then I thought I didn't want to look too eager, so I opted for a one-shoulder jumpsuit made in a beautiful green silk fabric. I paired it with some nice heels though comfortable enough to walk and dance without looking awkward.

 Aunty Elaine let me borrow her beautiful emerald earrings and helped me with my hair. She wanted to flat iron them but I told her I wanted to feel like myself tonight so we went for a more natural look. We put my hair into Bantu knots yesterday and today, after I finished up with my makeup, I took the knots out which created some very nice curls. I then picked it out a little at the base, so it turned out into a very cool afro. I added some big gold Bobbie pins in one side to finish the look.

I was ready to go. When I took the stairs down to the foyer, I saw Anthony talking with Uncle Eddie, his eyes lit up when he turned around and saw me.

 " I knew I had to step my game up tonight, you look gorgeous Ajia," he said giving me a kiss on my cheek.

"Well, I hope it's not too much. You haven't told me what kind of party we are going to. I'm very excited to spend the evening with you though. I see you have indeed stepped up your game." I said looking him up and then pointing my chin at his Cadillac escalade parked in front of the house.

We said goodbye to my aunt and uncle who were having their own date night, which I knew consists of watching some old French movies starring Gerard Depardieu. Uncle loves watching these movies while eating a nice takeaway and ice cream maybe some homemade toffee popcorn. My cousin Carlton and I loved these 'date nights', which we obviously crashed many times, me just cuddling on the sofa between aunty and uncle. Uncle would look pissed at first then they would both laugh it out.

Anthony and I drove down to Pine avenue pier. I don't know how he found out but this was my favorite thing about living in Long Beach: I love walking down the marina and enjoy the ocean breeze. Anthony made it even more special this evening when we boarded a nice yacht and sailed away from the dock just in time before sunset. While enjoying a glass of champagne, we watched as the sun got lower and lower the blue light scattered into red, orange and purple colors.
It was beautiful.
The chef, who turned out to be also the captain of the boat, then served us a delicious gourmet dinner. The atmosphere was lovely and we had so much to talk about. Just before dessert Anthony asked me for a dance, I was a little bit embarrassed but couldn't resist any longer. We swayed to the music or was it to the sound of the water? It felt like Time had stopped and we were alone in the world... Suddenly some

fireworks woke us up from our moment and we started to laugh like teenagers. The captain then came up to where we were dancing and announced that we were going to sail back to the dock.

After returning to the car, Anthony and I took the 710 freeway North to Torrance where the party was going to be. We couldn't find any parking close to the party house, not even the street behind, so Anthony said he would drop me at the door and then go find a space further up. Once we approached the front of the house, he called one of his homeboys, Kevin, on the phone and introduced me. He asked Kevin to take care of me until he comes back and drove off. Kevin and I walked inside the house where Usher's record "Yeah" was playing. I traced the loud sound to two huge speakers at the back of the house as Kevin was ushering me to where the dance floor and most of the guests were. Kevin told me the DJ was famous for his old school sets and asked if I needed anything. I told him not to worry about me (his phone kept ringing with people showing up at the door) I decided to head to the bar and get me a drink.

"Isn't she our future judge!"

"Liam! What a surprise! How are you?" I said as we hugged each other.

"I'm good. You look stunning. I didn't expect to see you in this part of town."

"Long Beach is only 20 minutes away. It's a nice party. I was just getting a drink I don't want to keep you from your friends we'll catch up later"

I didn't know what to say I just wanted to get away before Anthony arrives but...

"Here you are. I found a spot not too far away actually somebody was pulling out. You ok?" "Oh, Anthony you're back... Hmm yeah, I'm ok. I was..."

I was telling myself to think fast when I realized that feeling awkward would just make the situation worst. I was actually trapping myself into a crime that I wasn't guilty of. So, I told myself: 'No you are definitively not cheating;' maybe this was the awkward but perfect opportunity to introduce these two and make a full circle.

"I was catching up with an old friend. Anthony, this is Liam, Liam meet my date, Anthony."

Wedding day

Breathe, breathe. There we go some water, two deep breaths and I should be ok. Yes, it was my wedding day, I was still panicking but in a good way. Getting to this day was a journey and I wanted everything to be perfect even though Uncle Eddie repeatedly told me perfect weddings don't exist. I could write a whole new book about planning a wedding but I think it has already been done. The most challenging part for me was to feel like I had to 'look for my family.' I was even scared that on an administrative point of view we wouldn't be able to register our wedding because my biological mom and dad were not in my life.

I've never realized how much I was missing them, how important there were at this stage of my life. I guess, I was so fortunate to have Uncle Eddie and Aunty Elaine filling the void, so much than I have forgotten I was an orphan. It sounds horrible saying it out loud especially knowing that both of my parents were still alive. Well, Uncle strongly believed they were alive.

The beautiful thing with going through this and other issues that arose since we got engaged after dating for two years was that it felt like we had already knocked down the heavy rocks that could weight down our marriage in the long run. Or at least we've developed an open communication and deep understanding of each other that will help us overcome whatever comes our way. Of course, us both believing in God we would certainly put him at the core of our marital life.

Yes, I was anxious but with excitement because I couldn't wait to marry this man. I had never been so sure. Actually, I explained in detail the reason why I love him in the vows I have written. I stepped up closer to my husband-to-be ready to read my vows in front of the 200+ guest and more especially read it to him:

"Love is a feeling that is often taken lightly and when pushed to extreme some would tie it to hate. I have learned that the closer we are to God the better we are at loving others.   I love you because you make me want to be close to God. You have literally wooed me over and yet I don't have this fairy tale feeling. This feels real, I can feel the ground, I see your simplicity and admire it so much. You make me laugh shamelessly and not put on make-up some days just because. I want to be in your presence all the time.

Feel you, touch you, smell you.

We don't even have to talk. Our silence speaks louder about our attraction. And yet I can't help myself to tell you over and over how much I love you. Never know, in case you forget. I trust you, truly and entirely because I understand now that it's not just about feelings. I trust you because of your wonderful qualities, your God-fearing personality which is shown in every aspect of your life.

I have been observing you, the way you bite the tip of your pen, your crazy laugh, how sweet you are with others especially your family members. Every little thing that defines you, I have been taking it in before my feelings got too deep, just to see what kind of man you were and if I could bend my head to your leadership.   Your priorities and conception of life showed me that I don't have to:

I WANT TO.

Complete you and love you, until death do us part;

"Therefore, what God has yoked together, let no man put apart." (Matthew 19:6)

The End.

ABOUT THE AUTHOR

Reine was born in Suresnes, France. She studied English at the University of St Quentin-en-Yvelines (France). She then went to graduate school on an exchange program at the College of Charleston (USA) where she studied African American literature and African American studies while teaching French.

Later she moved to London (UK) where she obtained her Post Graduate Certificate in Education (PGCE) at Kingston University. She still enjoys a fulfilling career in Education while writing poems and short stories. This is her first self-published story.

Printed in Great Britain
by Amazon